AF406593

SKINCARE 101:

A COMPREHENSIVE GUIDE TO HEALTHY, GLOWING SKIN

BY
MASONWABE
NYANGA

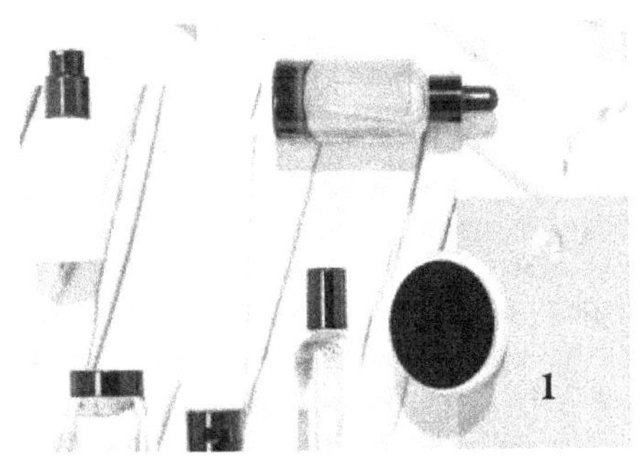

1

Acknowledgement:

I would like to express my gratitude to all the individuals who have contributed to the creation of this book. First and foremost, I would like to thank the countless skincare experts and enthusiasts who have shared their knowledge and insights with me. Your passion for healthy skin has been truly inspiring. I would also like to thank my friends and family for their unwavering support throughout this journey. Your encouragement and motivation kept me going when the going got tough. Special thanks to my editor and publisher for their guidance and expertise in helping me bring this project to life. Finally, I want to thank all the readers who have taken the time to read this book. I hope that it has provided you with the information and inspiration you need to take better care of your skin and achieve a healthy, glowing complexion.

Skincare 101: A Comprehensive Guide to Healthy, Glowing Skin

Introduction: The importance of taking care of your skin

Chapter 1: Understanding Your Skin Type

- Overview of different skin types
- How to determine your skin type
- Common skin concerns for each skin type

Chapter 2: Daily Skincare Routine for Healthy Skin

- The importance of a consistent skincare routine
- Step-by-step guide to a basic skincare routine
- Tips for incorporating additional skincare products
- Recommendations for morning and evening routines

Chapter 3: Common Skincare Mistakes to Avoid

- Overview of common skincare mistakes
- How to avoid these mistakes and improve your skincare routine
- The impact of lifestyle factors on your skin

Chapter 4: DIY Skincare Recipes for Natural Glow

- Benefits of using natural ingredients in skincare
- Recipes for homemade skincare products, including face masks, scrubs, and toners

Chapter 5: Skin Care for Specific Concerns

- Skincare tips and products for acne-prone skin
- Skincare tips and products for dry skin
- Skincare tips and products for oily skin
- Skincare tips and products for aging skin

Chapter 6: Skincare Products and Ingredients

- Overview of common skincare products and ingredients
- How to choose the right products for your skin type and concerns
- Understanding labels and ingredients lists

Conclusion: The importance of self-care and consistent skincare routine for healthy skin

By following the guidance and advice provided in Skincare 101, readers will have a comprehensive understanding of how to care for their skin and achieve a healthy, glowing complexion.

Introduction: The importance of taking care of your skin

Your skin is the largest organ in your body and serves as a barrier to protect you from environmental stressors, such as UV radiation and pollution. It also plays a crucial role in regulating body temperature, producing vitamin D, and providing sensory information.

Taking care of your skin is not just about achieving a beautiful complexion, but it also contributes to your overall health and well-being. Poor skin health can lead to a variety of issues, including acne, dryness, premature aging, and even skin cancer.

In this book, we will explore the importance of understanding your skin type, developing a daily skincare routine, avoiding common skincare mistakes, and using natural ingredients to achieve a healthy, glowing complexion. Whether you're a skincare novice or an experienced enthusiast, this guide will provide you with valuable information and practical tips to help you achieve your skincare goals.

Remember, everyone's skin is unique, and there is no one-size-fits-all solution to achieving healthy skin. By understanding your skin type and adopting healthy habits, you can create a personalized skincare routine that works best for you. Let's dive in and explore the world of skincare together.

When it comes to taking care of your skin, it's important to remember that it's not just about using the right products, but also about adopting healthy lifestyle habits. Factors such as diet, hydration, exercise, and sleep can all impact the health of your skin.

In addition, the skincare industry can be overwhelming with the vast array of products available, all promising to provide you with the perfect complexion. It's important to remember that not all products are created equal, and what works for one person may not work for another.

By understanding your skin type and its unique needs, you can make informed decisions when it comes to choosing skincare products and developing a routine. This book will provide you with the knowledge and tools necessary to make informed decisions about your skincare, so you can achieve healthy, glowing skin that you feel confident in.

Another important aspect of skincare is understanding the impact of external factors on your skin. Environmental stressors such as pollution, UV radiation, and harsh weather conditions can all take a toll on your skin's health and appearance. It's important to take steps to protect your skin from these factors, such as wearing sunscreen, using protective clothing, and avoiding prolonged exposure to the sun.

Moreover, stress and mental health can also impact the health of your skin. When you're stressed, your body produces more cortisol, which can lead to inflammation and breakouts. Practicing stress-reducing activities, such as meditation, yoga, or simply taking time for yourself, can have a positive impact on your skin's health.

Finally, skincare is not just about achieving a specific aesthetic outcome. It's about taking care of your body's largest organ and investing in your overall health and well-being. By taking the time to care for your skin, you're also taking care of yourself.

Chapter 1: Understanding Your Skin Type
• Overview of different skin types

There are generally five different skin types: normal, dry, oily, combination, and sensitive. Understanding your skin type is the first step in developing a skincare routine that works best for you. Here's an overview of each skin type:

There are generally five different skin types: normal, dry, oily, combination, and sensitive. Understanding your skin type is the first step in developing a skincare routine that works best for you. Here's an overview of each skin type:

1. **Normal skin:** This skin type has a balanced amount of oil and moisture, and generally has few imperfections. Normal skin is typically smooth, even toned, and has small pores.

2. **Dry skin:** Dry skin lacks moisture and can feel tight, itchy, and rough. This skin type may also be prone to flakiness, redness, and fine lines. Dry skin typically has small pores and may feel tight after cleansing.

3. **Oily skin:** Oily skin produces an excess amount of oil, which can lead to clogged pores, acne, and a shiny appearance. This skin type is typically thicker in texture and has larger pores.

4. **Combination skin:** Combination skin is a mix of both oily and dry skin. This skin type typically has an oily T-zone (forehead, nose, and chin) and dry cheeks. Combination skin may be prone to blackheads, whiteheads, and acne.

5. **Sensitive skin:** Sensitive skin is easily irritated by products, weather, and environmental factors. This skin type may be prone to redness, itching, and dryness.

In addition to the five main skin types, some people may also have specific skin conditions, such as acne-prone skin, rosacea, eczema, or psoriasis. These conditions may require specialized skincare routines and treatments.

It's important to note that while understanding your skin type is helpful, it's not the only factor to consider when developing a skincare routine. Factors such as age, gender, genetics, lifestyle, and environmental factors can also impact your skin's health and appearance.

Furthermore, it's possible to have more than one skin type, particularly in the case of combination skin. For example, you may have oily skin in some areas, such as the T-zone, but dry skin on the cheeks. In this case, it's important to tailor your skincare routine to meet the specific needs of each area of your face.

Ultimately, understanding your skin type and its unique needs is the first step in developing a skincare routine that works best for you. By taking the time to learn about your skin and adopting healthy habits, you can achieve healthy, glowing skin that you feel confident in.

• How to determine your skin type

Determining your skin type is important in developing an effective skincare routine. Here are some tips to help you determine your skin type:

1. **Normal skin:** Normal skin typically has a balanced amount of oil and moisture, with no signs of flakiness or excess oil. If your skin is smooth, even toned, and has small pores, you likely have normal skin.

2. **Dry skin:** If your skin feels tight, itchy, and looks flaky, you likely have dry skin. Dry skin may also appear dull and rough in texture.

1. **Oily skin:** Oily skin tends to produce excess oil, which can lead to clogged pores and a shiny appearance. If your skin feels greasy and appears shiny, particularly in the T-zone (forehead, nose, and chin), you likely have oily skin.

2. **Combination skin:** Combination skin is a mix of both dry and oily skin. If you have an oily T-zone but dry cheeks, you likely have combination skin.

3. **Sensitive skin:** Sensitive skin can be difficult to determine, as it can react to a variety of products and environmental factors. If your skin is easily irritated and prone to redness and itching, you may have sensitive skin.

To determine your skin type, start by washing your face with a gentle cleanser and patting it dry with a clean towel. Wait for 30 minutes without applying any products and observe how your skin feels and looks. If your skin feels balanced with no signs of dryness or oiliness, you likely have normal skin. If your skin feels tight, looks flaky, or has a dull appearance, you likely have dry skin. If your skin feels greasy and looks shiny, particularly in the T-zone, you likely have oily skin. If your skin has an oily T-zone but dry cheeks, you likely have combination skin. If your skin is easily irritated and prone to redness and itching, you may have sensitive skin.

Once you have determined your skin type, you can select skincare products and develop a routine that is tailored to your skin's unique needs.

It's important to keep in mind that your skin type may change over time, particularly as you age, experience hormonal changes, or are exposed to different environmental factors. It's a good idea to periodically re-evaluate your skin type to ensure that you are using the most effective products and routines.

In addition to the observation method described above, you can also consult with a dermatologist or esthetician to help determine your skin type. These professionals can perform a skin analysis using specialized equipment to measure factors such as oil production, hydration levels, and skin texture.

By determining your skin type and understanding its unique needs, you can select the most effective products and develop a skincare routine that helps to achieve healthy, glowing skin.

In addition to selecting the right skincare products and routine based on your skin type, it's also important to consider other factors that can impact your skin's health and appearance. These include:

1. **Age:** As we age, our skin becomes thinner and loses elasticity, leading to wrinkles and fine lines.
2. **Genetics:** Your genetics can play a role in your skin type and how it ages.
3. **Lifestyle:** Factors such as diet, exercise, stress, and smoking can impact your skin's health and appearance.
4. **Environment:** Exposure to pollution, sun damage, and other environmental factors can contribute to skin damage and premature aging.

SKINCARE 101: A COMPREHENSIVE GUIDE TO HEALTHY GLOWING SKIN

By taking a holistic approach to skincare, you can address these factors and promote overall skin health. This can include adopting healthy lifestyle habits, such as eating a balanced diet, staying hydrated, getting enough sleep, and managing stress. You can also protect your skin from environmental damage by wearing sunscreen, avoiding smoking, and limiting exposure to pollutants.

Understanding your skin type is an important first step in developing a skincare routine that promotes healthy, glowing skin. By considering other factors that can impact your skin's health and taking a holistic approach to skincare, you can achieve optimal skin health and appearance.

Another important factor to consider when it comes to skin health is the use of high-quality skincare products that are suited to your skin type and needs. Skincare products can help to nourish and protect your skin, while also addressing specific concerns such as acne, aging, and dryness.

When selecting skincare products, it's important to look for ingredients that are effective and safe for your skin type. For example, individuals with dry skin may benefit from using products that contain ingredients such as hyaluronic acid and ceramides, which help to lock in moisture. Those with oily skin may benefit from using products that contain salicylic acid, which can help to unclog pores and reduce oil production.

It's also important to be mindful of the quality and source of the skincare products you are using. Look for products that are made by reputable brands and free from potentially harmful ingredients such as parabens, sulfates, and fragrances.

Finally, consistency is key when it comes to skincare. Developing a daily skincare routine that includes cleansing, moisturizing, and protecting your skin can help to promote overall skin health and prevent issues such as acne and premature aging. By taking a holistic approach to skincare that considers your skin type, lifestyle factors, and the products you use, you can achieve healthy, glowing skin at any age.

• Common skin concerns for each skin type

Here are some common skin concerns for each skin type:

1. **Dry skin:** Dry skin is characterized by a lack of moisture and can feel tight, itchy, and rough. Common concerns for individuals with dry skin include flakiness, dullness, and fine lines and wrinkles.
2. **Oily skin:** Oily skin is characterized by an overproduction of sebum, the skin's natural oil, which can lead to a shiny, greasy appearance. Common concerns for individuals with oily skin include acne, blackheads, and enlarged pores.
3. **Combination skin:** Combination skin is characterized by both dry and oily areas, with the T-zone (forehead, nose, and chin) being typically oilier than the rest of the face. Common concerns for individuals with combination skin include oiliness in the T-zone, dryness in other areas of the face, and uneven skin tone.
4. **Normal skin:** Normal skin is well-balanced, with a healthy level of hydration and few noticeable concerns. However, even individuals with normal skin can experience issues such as dullness or uneven skin tone.
5. **Sensitive skin**: Sensitive skin is prone to irritation and can react negatively to certain ingredients or environmental factors. Common concerns for individuals with sensitive skin include redness, dryness, and flakiness.

It's important to note that these concerns can vary from person to person, even within the same skin type. If you are experiencing persistent or severe skin concerns, it's best to consult with a dermatologist or esthetician to determine the underlying cause and develop an effective treatment plan.

It's worth noting that some skin concerns may require more specialized or targeted treatments. For example, severe acne may require prescription-strength medications, while skin conditions such as rosacea or eczema may require specialized skincare products and/or medical treatments.

In addition to targeted treatments, there are also several general skincare practices that can help to promote healthy, vibrant skin. This includes protecting your skin from the sun by using sunscreen and wearing protective clothing, staying hydrated by drinking plenty of water, eating a balanced diet rich in fruits and vegetables, getting enough sleep, and avoiding smoking and excessive alcohol consumption.

Taking care of your skin involves a combination of understanding your skin type, being aware of potential skin concerns, adopting healthy lifestyle habits, and using quality skincare products that are suited to your needs. By prioritizing your skin's health and wellness, you can achieve a radiant, youthful complexion that reflects your overall wellbeing.

In the general skincare practices I mentioned earlier, there are also several other ways you can support the health and appearance of your skin. These include:

1. **Exfoliation:** Regular exfoliation can help to remove dead skin cells and promote cell turnover, which can improve the texture and tone of your skin. However, it's important to be gentle when exfoliating and avoid over-exfoliating, which can lead to irritation and sensitivity.

2. **Hydration:** Keeping your skin hydrated is crucial for maintaining its health and vitality. This can be achieved by using moisturizers and serums that are formulated to hydrate and nourish your skin, as well as drinking plenty of water

throughout the day.

3. **Stress management:** Stress can have a negative impact on your skin, leading to inflammation, breakouts, and other concerns. Finding ways to manage stress, such as through exercise, meditation, or other relaxation techniques, can help to support your skin's health and appearance.

4. **Professional treatments:** In addition to at-home skincare practices, there are also several professional treatments that can help to improve your skin's health and appearance. These may include facials, chemical peels, microdermabrasion, and other specialized treatments that can target specific concerns.

Ultimately, taking care of your skin is an ongoing process that requires attention, effort, and patience. By adopting healthy skincare practices and seeking professional guidance when needed, you can achieve the beautiful, radiant complexion you deserve.

It's also worth noting that some skincare ingredients can be particularly beneficial for certain skin types or concerns. For example, those with dry skin may benefit from using products that contain hyaluronic acid, which helps to hydrate and plump the skin. Those with oily skin may benefit from using products that contain salicylic acid, which helps to control oil production and prevent breakouts.

Other popular skincare ingredients include vitamin C, which can brighten and even out skin tone, and retinoids, which can improve the texture and appearance of the skin. However, it's important to be cautious when introducing new skincare ingredients into your routine, as some may be irritating or cause allergic reactions.

Finally, it's important to remember that skincare is not just about achieving a certain appearance or standard of beauty. Taking care of your skin is also about promoting your overall health and wellness and recognizing that your skin is a reflection of your internal wellbeing. By prioritizing your skin's health and taking care of yourself both inside and out, you can achieve a radiant, youthful complexion that reflects your overall vitality and wellbeing.

Another important aspect of skincare is being mindful of the environment and how our daily habits may impact the health of our skin. For example, exposure to pollution and other environmental toxins can lead to premature aging, uneven skin tone, and other skin concerns.

To mitigate the negative impact of environmental factors on our skin, it's important to take steps to protect our skin. This may include wearing a hat and protective clothing when spending time outside, using a physical sunscreen to protect against UV rays and pollution, and washing your face thoroughly at the end of the day to remove any pollutants or dirt that may have accumulated on your skin.

In addition to environmental factors, other lifestyle habits can also have an impact on the health and appearance of our skin. For example, smoking has been linked to premature aging and a dull, lackluster complexion, while excessive alcohol consumption can lead to dehydration and inflammation.

By being mindful of these environmental and lifestyle factors and taking steps to protect our skin, we can support its health and promote a youthful, radiant complexion. Ultimately, taking care of our skin is not just about achieving a certain look, but also about promoting our overall wellbeing and enjoying healthy, glowing skin for years to come.

Chapter 2: Daily Skincare Routine for Healthy Skin

• The importance of a consistent skincare routine

Having a consistent skincare routine is crucial for maintaining the health and appearance of your skin. Just like any other aspect of your health, taking care of your skin requires regular attention and effort.

A consistent skincare routine can help to address a range of skin concerns, including acne, dryness, wrinkles, and hyperpigmentation. By using products that are tailored to your skin type and concerns, you can help to address these issues and promote the overall health of your skin.

Moreover, a consistent skincare routine can help to prevent future skin concerns from arising. By taking a proactive approach to skincare, you can help to protect your skin from damage and maintain its health and vitality over the long term.

Consistency is also key when it comes to seeing results from your skincare routine. While some skincare products may provide immediate benefits, many require consistent use over time in order to see real improvements. By sticking to a consistent routine, you can maximize the benefits of your skincare products and achieve the best possible results for your skin.

A consistent skincare routine is an essential part of maintaining healthy, radiant skin. By making skincare a priority and establishing a routine that works for you, you can help to achieve the beautiful, youthful complexion you deserve.

The benefits mentioned earlier, having a consistent skincare routine can also have a positive impact on your mental wellbeing. Taking the time to care for your skin can be a form of self-care and can help you feel more confident and refreshed.

SKINCARE 101: A COMPREHENSIVE GUIDE TO HEALTHY GLOWING SKIN

Moreover, establishing a consistent skincare routine can help to simplify your life by streamlining your beauty routine. By having a set routine, you can avoid the confusion and overwhelm that can come with using too many products or constantly switching between different skincare routines.

When establishing a skincare routine, it's important to keep in mind that every person's skin is unique and may require a different approach. What works for one person may not work for another, so it's important to pay attention to your skin's specific needs and adjust your routine accordingly.

Overall, the key to a successful skincare routine is consistency, patience, and flexibility. By taking a mindful, proactive approach to skincare and establishing a routine that works for you, you can achieve healthy, radiant skin and feel confident and beautiful in your own skin.

It's also worth noting that a consistent skincare routine doesn't have to be complicated or time-consuming. You can establish a basic routine that includes just a few key steps, such as cleansing, moisturizing, and applying sunscreen. As you become more comfortable with your routine, you can incorporate additional products or steps as needed.

It's also important to keep in mind that skincare isn't just about the products you use, but also about your overall lifestyle habits. Factors such as diet, exercise, and stress management can all impact the health and appearance of your skin. By taking a holistic approach to skincare and incorporating healthy habits into your daily routine, you can support the overall health of your skin and achieve a radiant, youthful complexion.

Ultimately, the key to a successful skincare routine is finding what works for you and sticking with it. Whether you prefer a simple routine or a more elaborate one, consistency is key. With time, patience, and a little bit of experimentation, you can establish a skincare routine that supports the health and beauty of your skin for years to come.

It's also important to note that while consistency is key, it's also important to be flexible and adaptable when it comes to your skincare routine. Your skin's needs may change over time, particularly in response to factors such as aging, hormonal fluctuations, and changes in the environment.

As such, it's important to pay attention to your skin's specific needs and adjust your routine as needed. This may mean incorporating new products, switching up your cleansing or exfoliation routine, or adjusting the frequency with which you use certain products.

It's also important to note that skincare is not a one-size-fits-all approach. What works for one person may not work for another, and it may take some trial and error to find the products and routine that work best for your skin.

It's important to approach skincare with a mindset of self-care and self-love, rather than as a means to achieve a certain standard of beauty. Everyone's skin is unique, and there is no "perfect" or "ideal" complexion. Rather than striving for perfection, focus on nourishing and caring for your skin in a way that feels good to you.

In summary, establishing a consistent skincare routine is crucial for maintaining the health and appearance of your skin. However, it's important to approach skincare with flexibility and adaptability, and to focus on self-care and self-love rather than striving for a certain standard of beauty. With time, patience, and a mindful approach, you can achieve healthy, radiant skin that makes you feel confident and beautiful.

• Step-by-step guide to a basic skincare routine

Step-by-step guide to a basic skincare routine that can be customized based on your skin type and concerns:

1. **Cleanse:** The first step in any skincare routine is to cleanse your skin to remove dirt, oil, and impurities. Choose a gentle, non-foaming cleanser that is appropriate for your skin type, and massage it into your skin using gentle circular motions. Rinse thoroughly with lukewarm water and pat your skin dry with a clean towel.
2. **Tone:** After cleansing, use a toner to help balance the pH of your skin and prepare it for the rest of your skincare routine. Apply the toner to a cotton pad and sweep it over your face, avoiding the eye area.
3. **Treat:** If you have specific skin concerns such as acne, hyperpigmentation, or fine lines, you may want to use a targeted treatment product such as a serum or spot treatment. Apply the treatment product to your face and neck using gentle upward strokes.
4. **Moisturize:** Next, apply a moisturizer to your face and neck to hydrate and nourish your skin. Choose a moisturizer that is appropriate for your skin type and apply it using gentle upward strokes.
5. **Protect:** Finally, apply a broad-spectrum sunscreen with an SPF of at least 30 to protect your skin from harmful UV rays. Apply it liberally to your face and neck and reapply throughout the day as needed.

Remember, this is just a basic skincare routine, and you may need to adjust it based on your skin type and concerns. Additionally, you may choose to incorporate additional steps such as exfoliation, masks, or eye cream into your routine as needed. With time and experimentation, you can develop a skincare routine that works best for you and helps you achieve healthy, radiant skin.

It's important to note that the consistency of your skincare routine can make a big difference in the health and appearance of your skin. Consistency is key when it comes to seeing results and maintaining healthy skin. It's recommended to follow this basic routine every morning and night, and to stick with it for at least a few weeks to see improvements.

So It's important to choose skincare products that are appropriate for your skin type and concerns. For example, if you have oily skin, you may want to choose lightweight, oil-free products, while if you have dry skin, you may want to choose richer, more hydrating products. It's also important to patch test any new products before incorporating them into your routine to make sure they don't cause irritation or allergic reactions.

Finally, it's important to remember that skincare is not a one-size-fits-all solution. Everyone's skin is different, and what works for one person may not work for another. It's important to listen to your skin and adjust your routine as needed to achieve the best results.

It's also worth mentioning that there are certain lifestyle factors that can impact the health of your skin, and incorporating these habits into your routine can help you achieve healthy, glowing skin from the inside out. These habits include:

1. **Staying hydrated:** Drinking plenty of water can help keep your skin hydrated and healthy.
2. **Eating a balanced diet:** Eating a diet rich in fruits, vegetables, whole grains, and lean proteins can provide your skin with the nutrients it needs to stay healthy.
3. **Getting enough sleep:** Lack of sleep can contribute to dull,

tired-looking skin, so it's important to aim for 7-8 hours of sleep per night.

4. **Managing stress:** Stress can cause breakouts and other skin issues, so it's important to find healthy ways to manage stress, such as exercise, meditation, or spending time in nature.

By incorporating these habits into your routine, along with a consistent skincare routine, you can help achieve healthy, glowing skin that looks and feels its best.

It's also important to note that while a basic skincare routine can help maintain the health of your skin, there may be times when you need to adjust or add to your routine to address specific skin concerns. For example, if you're dealing with acne or hyperpigmentation, you may want to incorporate additional products such as spot treatments or serums that target these concerns.

In addition, as you age, your skin's needs may change, and you may need to adjust your skincare routine accordingly. For example, as you get older, your skin may become drier and more prone to wrinkles, so you may want to incorporate richer, more hydrating products into your routine.

The key to achieving healthy, radiant skin is to be consistent with your skincare routine, listen to your skin's needs, and be willing to adjust your routine as needed to achieve the best results. With the right products and habits, you can help keep your skin looking and feeling its best for years to come.

• Tips for incorporating additional skincare products

Incorporating additional skincare products into your routine can be a great way to address specific skin concerns, but it's important to do so carefully to avoid irritating or damaging your skin. Here are some tips for adding new products to your routine:

1. **Introduce new products gradually:** It's important to introduce new products slowly, one at a time, to allow your skin to adjust and to monitor any potential reactions or irritation. Start by using the new product every other day or a few times a week, and gradually increase to daily use as your skin tolerates it.
2. **Follow the instructions:** Be sure to follow the instructions on the product label, including how much to use and how often to apply it.
3. **Be patient:** It can take time to see results from new products, so be patient and stick with it for at least a few weeks before deciding if it's working for you.

1. **Patch test:** Always patch test new products on a small area of skin before applying them all over your face to make sure you don't have an allergic reaction or sensitivity.
2. **Use products in the right order:** It's important to apply products in the right order to get the most benefit from each one. Generally, you'll want to apply products in order of thickness, starting with the thinnest product and ending with the thickest.
3. **Be mindful of interactions:** Some skincare products can interact with each other, so it's important to be mindful of how different products work together. For example, using retinol

and AHAs/BHAs together can be too harsh for some skin types, so it's best to alternate them or use them on different days.

By following these tips, you can safely and effectively incorporate additional skincare products into your routine to help address specific skin concerns and achieve your best skin.

It's important to note that not all skincare products are created equal, and it's important to choose products that are appropriate for your skin type and concerns. If you're unsure which products to use or how to use them, it can be helpful to consult with a skincare professional, such as a dermatologist or licensed esthetician, who can provide personalized recommendations based on your skin type and concerns.

It's important to be mindful of the ingredients in your skincare products, especially if you have sensitive skin. Some common skincare ingredients, such as fragrances and certain preservatives, can cause irritation or allergic reactions in some people. If you have sensitive skin, look for products that are labeled as fragrance-free or hypoallergenic, and avoid products that contain known irritants.

Finally, it's important to remember that skincare is just one aspect of overall health and wellness. A healthy diet, regular exercise, and getting enough sleep can all contribute to healthy, radiant skin. By taking care of your body both inside and out, you can help maintain the health and appearance of your skin for years to come.

• Recommendations for morning and evening routines

Morning routine:

1. **Cleanser:** Use a gentle cleanser to remove any oil, sweat, or bacteria that may have accumulated on your skin overnight.
2. **Toner:** Apply a toner to balance your skin's pH levels and prep your skin for the rest of your routine.
3. **Serum:** Apply a serum with antioxidants, such as vitamin C, to protect your skin from environmental stressors like pollution and UV rays.
4. **Eye cream:** Apply a moisturizing eye cream to hydrate and brighten the delicate skin around your eyes.
5. **Moisturizer:** Apply a lightweight moisturizer to lock in hydration and keep your skin looking healthy and glowing.
6. **Sunscreen:** Finish with a broad-spectrum sunscreen with at least SPF 30 to protect your skin from harmful UV rays.

Evening routine:

1. **Cleansing oil/balm:** Use a cleansing oil or balm to remove makeup, sunscreen, and other impurities.
2. **Cleanser:** Follow up with a gentle cleanser to remove any remaining dirt and oil.
3. Toner: Apply a toner to balance your skin's pH levels and prep your skin for the rest of your routine.
4. **Exfoliant:** Use an exfoliating product, such as a chemical exfoliant or a scrub, to remove dead skin cells and improve skin texture.
5. **Serum:** Apply a serum with active ingredients, such as retinol, to target specific skin concerns like fine lines or acne.

6. **Eye cream:** Apply a moisturizing eye cream to hydrate and brighten the delicate skin around your eyes.

1. **Moisturizer:** Apply a heavier moisturizer than your morning routine to lock in hydration while you sleep.

Of course, these are just general recommendations, and you should tailor your skincare routine to your skin type and specific concerns. If you have any questions or concerns, it's always a good idea to consult with a skincare professional.

It's important to note that not everyone needs to follow an extensive skincare routine with multiple steps. Some people may find that a simple routine of just a cleanser, moisturizer, and sunscreen works best for their skin. On the other hand, some people may need to incorporate additional products like serums, toners, or masks to address specific skin concerns.

It's also important to be patient when trying out new skincare products. It can take time for your skin to adjust to new ingredients, and you may not see immediate results. It's recommended to introduce new products slowly, one at a time, and give your skin a few weeks to adjust before adding anything else.

It's important to pay attention to how your skin reacts to different products and adjust your routine accordingly. If you notice any irritation, redness, or breakouts, it may be a sign that a product isn't right for your skin.

A consistent skincare routine tailored to your specific skin type and concerns can help keep your skin healthy, hydrated, and glowing.

Chapter 3: Common Skincare Mistakes to Avoid

• Overview of common skincare mistakes

Skincare mistakes are easy to make, and they can harm your skin rather than help it. Here are some of the most common skincare mistakes to avoid:

1. **Over-washing your face:** Over-washing your face can strip your skin of its natural oils and lead to dryness, irritation, and breakouts. It's best to wash your face no more than twice a day, using a gentle cleanser.
2. **Using hot water to wash your face:** Hot water can also strip your skin of its natural oils and cause dryness and irritation. It's best to use lukewarm water when washing your face.
3. **Not removing your makeup before bed:** Leaving your makeup on overnight can clog your pores and lead to breakouts. It's important to remove your makeup before going to bed, using a gentle makeup remover.
4. **Using too many products at once:** Using too many skincare products can overload your skin and cause irritation and breakouts. It's best to keep your routine simple and only use products that are necessary for your skin type and concerns.
5. **Skipping sunscreen:** Sun damage can lead to premature aging, sunspots, and skin cancer. It's important to wear sunscreen every day, even on cloudy days.
6. **Touching your face:** Touching your face can transfer bacteria from your hands to your face, leading to breakouts and irritation. It's best to avoid touching your face as much as possible.

By avoiding these common skincare mistakes, you can help keep your skin healthy, clear, and glowing.

It's also important to note that everyone's skin is unique, and what works for one person may not work for another. It's essential to listen to your skin and adjust your routine accordingly. If you notice any irritation, redness, or breakouts, it may be a sign that you need to change your skincare routine or eliminate a specific product.

Another common mistake is to use products that are too harsh for your skin type. If you have sensitive skin, using products that contain harsh ingredients like alcohol, fragrance, or exfoliants can lead to irritation and redness. It's best to look for products that are formulated specifically for your skin type and are gentle on your skin.

Additionally, it's important to follow the instructions on each skincare product and not to overuse them. Using too much of a product can lead to irritation, dryness, and even acne.

In summary, avoiding these common skincare mistakes and following a consistent and personalized skincare routine can help you achieve healthy, glowing skin.

Another common mistake people make is not properly removing their makeup before going to bed. Sleeping with makeup on can clog pores, lead to breakouts, and prevent the skin from properly rejuvenating overnight. It's essential to thoroughly cleanse your skin before bed, even if you didn't wear makeup during the day.

Another mistake is using hot water to wash your face. Hot water can strip your skin of its natural oils, leading to dryness and irritation. Instead, use lukewarm water to cleanse your face and avoid scrubbing your skin too hard, as this can also lead to irritation and redness.

Many people also make the mistake of not using sunscreen regularly. Sun damage is one of the leading causes of premature aging, wrinkles, and skin cancer. It's essential to protect your skin from the sun's harmful UV rays by wearing sunscreen daily, even on cloudy days.

Lastly, some people tend to switch up their skincare routine too frequently, which can be detrimental to their skin. It's best to introduce new products one at a time and gradually incorporate them into your routine. This way, you can determine whether a particular product is working for you or not and avoid overwhelming your skin with too many new products at once.

• How to avoid these mistakes and improve your skincare routine

To avoid common skincare mistakes and improve your routine, it's essential to understand your skin type and its unique needs. Once you determine your skin type, you can look for products that are formulated specifically for your skin and avoid products that are too harsh or contain irritating ingredients.

It's also important to follow a consistent skincare routine that includes cleansing, toning, moisturizing, and protecting your skin from the sun's harmful UV rays. Make sure to use a gentle cleanser, apply toner to balance your skin's pH levels, and use a moisturizer to keep your skin hydrated.

Incorporate additional skincare products like serums and masks gradually, one at a time, and observe how your skin reacts to them. This way, you can determine which products work for you and which ones to avoid.

Finally, it's essential to pay attention to your skin and adjust your routine accordingly. If you notice any irritation, redness, or breakouts, consider eliminating a particular product from your routine or changing the frequency of use. Don't be afraid to consult a dermatologist if you're struggling with persistent skin issues or need additional guidance on your skincare routine.

It's also important to keep in mind that a healthy lifestyle can have a significant impact on your skin's health. Eating a well-balanced diet, staying hydrated, getting enough sleep, and managing stress can all contribute to healthy, glowing skin.

Another common mistake is over-exfoliating or using harsh exfoliating products. While exfoliating can help remove dead skin cells and unclog pores, overdoing it can damage your skin's protective barrier and lead to irritation, dryness, and sensitivity. It's best to exfoliate no more than once or twice a week and use a gentle exfoliator.

Additionally, neglecting to protect your skin from the sun's harmful UV rays is a common mistake that can lead to premature aging, dark spots, and even skin cancer. It's essential to use a broad-spectrum sunscreen with at least SPF 30 every day, even when it's cloudy or you're indoors.

By understanding common skincare mistakes and taking steps to avoid them, you can improve the overall health and appearance of your skin. A consistent skincare routine that caters to your skin's unique needs, coupled with a healthy lifestyle, can lead to a healthy, glowing complexion.

Incorporating professional treatments and seeking advice from a dermatologist or esthetician can also help you avoid skincare mistakes and achieve optimal skin health. They can provide personalized recommendations for your skin type and address any specific concerns you may have.

It's important to remember that skincare is not a one-size-fits-all approach. What works for one person may not work for another, and it can take time to find the right products and routine for your skin. Be patient, and don't be afraid to experiment and try new things until you find what works best for you.

It's essential to have realistic expectations when it comes to skincare. While a good skincare routine can improve the appearance of your skin, it won't magically fix all of your skin concerns overnight. Consistency is key, and with time and patience, you can achieve healthy, glowing skin.

The impact of lifestyle factors on your skin

Your lifestyle habits can have a significant impact on the health and appearance of your skin. Here are some examples:

1. **Diet:** Eating a diet high in processed foods, sugar, and unhealthy fats can lead to inflammation in the body, which can manifest on the skin in the form of acne, wrinkles, and dullness. Eating a well-balanced diet rich in fruits, vegetables, lean proteins, and healthy fats can provide your skin with the nutrients it needs to look its best.
2. **Hydration:** Staying hydrated is crucial for healthy skin. When you're dehydrated, your skin can appear dry, flaky, and dull. Drinking enough water can help keep your skin plump, moisturized, and glowing.
3. **Sleep:** Getting enough sleep is essential for skin health. When you don't get enough sleep, your body releases stress hormones that can lead to inflammation and breakouts. Aim for at least 7-8 hours of sleep per night to keep your skin looking its best.
4. **Stress:** Chronic stress can wreak havoc on your skin, leading to inflammation, breakouts, and premature aging. Finding ways to manage stress, such as through exercise, meditation, or therapy, can help keep your skin healthy and glowing.
5. **Sun exposure:** Too much sun exposure can cause damage to the skin, leading to wrinkles, dark spots, and an increased risk of skin cancer. Wearing a broad-spectrum sunscreen with at least SPF 30 every day, avoiding midday sun, and wearing protective clothing can all help protect your skin from the sun's harmful rays.

By adopting healthy lifestyle habits and taking care of your skin through a consistent skincare routine, you can help your skin look and feel its best.

There are other external factors that can impact the health and appearance of your skin. These include:

1. **Environmental pollutants:** Exposure to pollutants such as smog, cigarette smoke, and car exhaust can cause oxidative stress in the skin, leading to premature aging and other skin concerns.
2. **Harsh skincare products:** Using skincare products that contain harsh chemicals or fragrances can irritate the skin, leading to redness, inflammation, and breakouts.
3. **Over-exfoliation:** Over-exfoliating the skin can strip away its natural oils and disrupt the skin barrier, leading to dryness, sensitivity, and irritation.
4. **Picking at blemishes:** Picking at blemishes can cause further inflammation and can even lead to scarring.

To protect your skin from these external factors, it's important to choose gentle skincare products that are appropriate for your skin type and to avoid over-exfoliating or using harsh products. It's also important to protect your skin from the sun and environmental pollutants by wearing protective clothing and using a broad-spectrum sunscreen daily.

Taking care of your skin requires a holistic approach that involves adopting healthy lifestyle habits, using gentle and effective skincare products, and protecting your skin from external factors that can cause damage.

In addition to the external factors, internal factors such as stress and lack of sleep can also have a significant impact on the health of your skin. When you're stressed, your body produces more cortisol, a hormone that can increase oil production in the skin and lead to breakouts. Lack of sleep can also lead to increased inflammation in the body, which can exacerbate skin conditions such as acne and eczema.

To support the health of your skin from the inside out, it's important to prioritize stress management techniques such as exercise, meditation, or deep breathing. Getting enough sleep and maintaining a healthy diet rich in vitamins, antioxidants, and essential fatty acids can also help support skin health.

It's important to remember that everyone's skin is unique, and what works for one person may not work for another. It may take some trial and error to find the right skincare routine and lifestyle habits that work for you and your skin. However, by adopting a holistic approach to skincare and being mindful of the internal and external factors that can impact your skin, you can achieve healthy, glowing skin that looks and feels its best.

Lack of sleep, and diet, other lifestyle factors can also impact your skin. For example, smoking cigarettes can lead to premature aging, dryness, and dullness of the skin. Sun exposure can also have a significant impact on the health of your skin, as it can lead to sunburn, wrinkles, and even skin cancer.

To protect your skin from the harmful effects of the sun, it's important to wear sunscreen every day, even on cloudy days. Look for a broad-spectrum sunscreen with an SPF of 30 or higher and reapply it every two hours if you're outside. Wearing protective clothing such as hats and long-sleeved shirts can also help protect your skin from the sun's harmful rays.

In summary, taking care of your skin involves more than just a skincare routine. It also involves being mindful of the lifestyle factors that can impact your skin, such as stress, lack of sleep, diet, smoking, and sun exposure. By adopting healthy habits and being mindful of these factors, you can support the health of your skin and achieve a radiant, healthy glow.

Chapter 4: DIY Skincare Recipes for Natural Glow

• Benefits of using natural ingredients in skincare

There are several benefits to using natural ingredients in skincare products. Here are a few:

1. **Gentle on the skin:** Natural ingredients are often less harsh and abrasive than synthetic ingredients, making them gentler on the skin.
2. **Fewer irritations:** Natural ingredients are less likely to cause allergic reactions or irritations, making them a great choice for those with sensitive skin.
3. **Nourishing and hydrating:** Many natural ingredients are rich in vitamins, minerals, and antioxidants that can nourish and hydrate the skin.
4. **Eco-friendly:** Natural ingredients are often more sustainable and eco-friendly than synthetic ones, which can be harmful to the environment.
5. **Cost-effective:** Natural ingredients can often be found at a lower cost than synthetic ones, making them a cost-effective option for those on a budget.

Some popular natural ingredients in skincare include aloe vera, coconut oil, tea tree oil, jojoba oil, shea butter, and chamomile. However, it's important to note that not all natural ingredients are safe or effective for everyone, so it's important to do your research and patch test new products before incorporating them into your skincare routine.

Using natural ingredients in skincare can also have a positive impact on your overall health and well-being. Many synthetic ingredients in skincare products can be absorbed through the skin and enter your bloodstream, potentially causing harm to your body. In contrast, natural ingredients are generally safer and less toxic, reducing the risk of harmful side effects.

Additionally, natural skincare products are often cruelty-free, meaning they are not tested on animals. This can be an important consideration for those who are concerned about animal welfare and want to ensure that their skincare products align with their values.

Finally, using natural ingredients in skincare can be a fun and creative way to experiment with different combinations and formulations. There are countless natural ingredients with different properties and benefits, so you can tailor your skincare routine to your specific needs and preferences. incorporating natural ingredients into your skincare routine can be a great way to promote healthy, glowing skin while also supporting your values and lifestyle.

Another benefit of using natural ingredients in skincare is that they are often more environmentally friendly than synthetic alternatives. Many synthetic skincare ingredients can be harmful to the environment, particularly when they are washed down the drain and end up in our waterways. In contrast, natural ingredients are often biodegradable and sustainable, meaning they are less likely to cause harm to the planet.

Furthermore, natural ingredients can be more affordable than their synthetic counterparts. Many natural ingredients can be found in your kitchen or at your local grocery store, making them accessible and cost-effective. This can be particularly beneficial for those who are on a budget or prefer to use simple, natural products in their skincare routine.

The benefits of using natural ingredients in skincare are numerous and varied. From promoting healthy skin to supporting your values and lifestyle, incorporating natural ingredients into your skincare routine can be a great way to achieve beautiful, radiant skin while also promoting a more sustainable and ethical approach to personal care.

Natural ingredients can be gentler on the skin than synthetic alternatives. Many synthetic skincare ingredients can be harsh and irritating to the skin, especially for those with sensitive skin. Natural ingredients, on the other hand, are typically milder and less likely to cause adverse reactions. This can make them a great choice for individuals with sensitive or allergy-prone skin.

Natural ingredients can also provide a range of benefits for different skin concerns. For example, honey is a natural humectant, which means it helps to draw moisture to the skin and can be especially beneficial for dry or dehydrated skin. Tea tree oil is a natural antibacterial and can be helpful for treating acne-prone skin. And green tea contains antioxidants that can help to protect the skin from environmental damage and promote a more youthful, radiant complexion.

Another advantage of using natural ingredients is that they can be more nourishing and supportive for the skin over the long term. Synthetic ingredients may provide short-term benefits, but they can also be drying or damaging to the skin over time. Natural ingredients, on the other hand, can help to support the skin's natural function and promote healthy, balanced skin in the long run.

• Recipes for homemade skincare products, including face masks, scrubs, and toners

Here are a few simple recipes for homemade skincare products:

1. **Honey and Oatmeal Face Mask:** Mix together 1/4 cup of ground oatmeal, 2 tablespoons of honey, and enough water to create a paste. Apply the mask to your face and let it sit for 10-15 minutes before rinsing off with warm water. This mask is great for soothing and hydrating the skin.

2. **Brown Sugar and Olive Oil Scrub:** Mix together 1/4 cup of brown sugar and 2 tablespoons of olive oil. Apply the mixture to your skin in a gentle, circular motion, then rinse off with warm water. This scrub is great for exfoliating and moisturizing the skin.

3. **Green Tea Toner:** Brew a cup of green tea and let it cool completely. Transfer the tea to a spray bottle and mist it over your face after cleansing. Green tea is rich in antioxidants and can help to soothe and protect the skin.

4. **Avocado and Yogurt Face Mask:** Mash 1/2 of a ripe avocado and mix it with 2 tablespoons of plain yogurt. Apply the mixture to your face and let it sit for 10-15 minutes before rinsing off with warm water. This mask is great for nourishing and brightening the skin.

5. **Aloe Vera and Witch Hazel Toner:** Mix together 1/4 cup of aloe vera gel and 1/4 cup of witch hazel. Transfer the mixture to a spray bottle and mist it over your face after cleansing. Aloe vera is soothing and hydrating, while witch hazel can help to tighten and tone the skin.

These are just a few examples of the many homemade skincare products you can create using natural ingredients. Be sure to patch test any new products on a small area of skin before using them all over your face and consult with a dermatologist if you have any concerns or underlying skin conditions.

Homemade skincare products can be a fun and cost-effective way to incorporate natural ingredients into your skincare routine. Here are a few examples of recipes you can try at home:

1. **Honey and oatmeal face mask:** Mix one tablespoon of honey with one tablespoon of ground oatmeal to create a paste. Apply the paste to your face and let it sit for 10-15 minutes before rinsing off with warm water.
2. **Coffee body scrub**: Mix 1/2 cup of ground coffee with 1/2 cup of coconut oil and 1/4 cup of brown sugar. Use the mixture to scrub your body in the shower, focusing on dry areas like elbows and knees.
3. **Green tea toner:** Brew a cup of green tea and let it cool. Transfer the tea to a spray bottle and spritz it onto your face after cleansing.
4. **Avocado and banana hair mask:** Mash one ripe avocado and one ripe banana together, then apply the mixture to your hair. Leave the mask on for 30 minutes before rinsing out with shampoo.

These are just a few examples of the many DIY skincare recipes out there. When making your own products, be sure to research the ingredients thoroughly and test them on a small patch of skin before applying them all over your face or body.

When it comes to creating homemade skincare products, there are a plethora of ingredients to choose from, including natural oils, fruits, vegetables, and herbs. Here are a few examples of DIY skincare recipes:

SKINCARE 101: A COMPREHENSIVE GUIDE TO HEALTHY GLOWING SKIN

1. **Honey and Oatmeal Face Mask:** Mix 1 tablespoon of honey with 1 tablespoon of finely ground oatmeal. Apply the mixture to your face and leave it on for 15 minutes before rinsing off with warm water. This mask can help soothe and moisturize the skin.

2. **Coconut Oil and Brown Sugar Scrub:** Mix 1/2 cup of coconut oil with 1/2 cup of brown sugar. Apply the mixture to your skin and gently massage in circular motions. Rinse off with warm water. This scrub can help exfoliate and hydrate the skin.

3. **Green Tea Toner:** Brew a cup of green tea and let it cool. Pour the tea into a spray bottle and spritz it onto your face after cleansing. Green tea is rich in antioxidants and can help reduce inflammation and redness.

4. **Avocado and Banana Face Mask:** Mash 1/2 ripe avocado and 1/2 ripe banana together. Apply the mixture to your face and leave it on for 10-15 minutes before rinsing off with warm water. This mask can help nourish and hydrate the skin.

It's important to keep in mind that not all natural ingredients are suitable for every skin type, and some may even cause allergic reactions. It's a good idea to do a patch test before applying any new ingredient to your skin and to consult with a dermatologist if you have any concerns.

Chapter 5: Skin Care for Specific Concerns

• Skincare tips and products for acne-prone skin

Acne-prone skin can be frustrating to deal with, but with the right skincare routine and products, it is possible to keep breakouts under control. Here are some tips and products that can be helpful for acne-prone skin:

1. **Use a gentle cleanser**: Look for a cleanser that is gentle and doesn't strip your skin of its natural oils. Avoid using harsh soaps or scrubbing your skin too hard, as this can cause irritation and make acne worse.

2. **Choose non-comedogenic products:** Non-comedogenic products are specifically formulated not to clog pores. Look for this label on your skincare and makeup products to avoid further breakouts.

3. **Exfoliate regularly:** Exfoliation can help to remove dead skin cells that can clog pores and lead to breakouts. However, be careful not to over-exfoliate, as this can irritate your skin and make acne worse. Aim to exfoliate 1-2 times per week with a gentle exfoliant.

4. **Use a spot treatment:** Spot treatments can help to target individual pimples and speed up the healing process. Look for products containing benzoyl peroxide, salicylic acid, or tea tree oil, which are all effective at fighting acne.

5. **Moisturize daily:** It's important to keep your skin hydrated, even if you have acne-prone skin. Look for a lightweight, oil-free moisturizer that won't clog pores.

6. **Protect your skin from the sun:** Sun damage can make acne scars worse, so it's important to protect your skin with a broad-spectrum sunscreen. Look for a non-comedogenic sunscreen with an SPF of at least 30.

Some recommended products for acne-prone skin include:

- Cetaphil Daily Facial Cleanser
- Neutrogena Oil-Free Acne Wash
- Paula's Choice Skin Perfecting 2% BHA Liquid Exfoliant
- Mario Badescu Drying Lotion
- La Roche-Posay Effaclar Duo Acne Treatment
- The Ordinary Niacinamide 10% + Zinc 1%
- EltaMD UV Clear Facial Sunscreen

Remember, everyone's skin is unique, so it may take some trial and error to find the products that work best for you. If you're struggling with acne, it's also a good idea to consult with a dermatologist for personalized advice and treatment options.

Acne-prone skin can be challenging to manage, but with the right skincare tips and products, you can minimize breakouts and achieve healthier-looking skin. Here are some tips to keep in mind:

1. **Cleansing:** Use a gentle cleanser twice a day to remove excess oil and dirt from the skin. Avoid harsh scrubbing or using hot water, as this can irritate the skin and worsen acne.
2. **Exfoliation:** Exfoliate once or twice a week to remove dead skin cells and unclog pores. Look for products that contain salicylic acid or benzoyl peroxide, which can help treat acne.
3. **Moisturizing:** Even if you have oily skin, it's important to moisturize daily to keep the skin hydrated and healthy. Look for lightweight, oil-free moisturizers that won't clog pores.
4. **Sun protection:** Protect your skin from the sun's harmful UV

rays by using a broad-spectrum sunscreen with an SPF of 30 or higher. Sunscreen can also help prevent post-inflammatory hyperpigmentation (PIH) or dark spots caused by acne.

5. **Avoid touching your face:** Touching your face can transfer bacteria and oil to your skin, which can worsen acne. Keep your hands away from your face as much as possible and avoid picking or popping pimples.
6. **Use non-comedogenic products:** Choose skincare and makeup products that are labeled non-comedogenic, which means they won't clog pores.
7. **Seek professional help:** If your acne is severe or persistent, consider seeing a dermatologist who can prescribe medications or recommend other treatments, such as chemical peels or laser therapy.

There are also many over-the-counter skincare products that can help treat acne. Look for products that contain active ingredients such as salicylic acid, benzoyl peroxide, or retinoids. However, be cautious of overusing these products, as they can cause dryness and irritation if used excessively.

Ultimately, finding the right skincare routine for acne-prone skin may take some trial and error. Be patient and consistent, and don't hesitate to seek professional help if needed.

Acne-prone skin is a common concern for many people, and it can be frustrating to deal with. However, there are several tips and products that can help improve the appearance of acne and prevent future breakouts.

First and foremost, it's important to establish a consistent skincare routine that includes gentle cleansing and moisturizing. Look for products that are labeled as "non-comedogenic" or "oil-free" to avoid clogging pores.

In addition, incorporating a salicylic acid or benzoyl peroxide product into your routine can help unclog pores and reduce inflammation associated with acne. However, be cautious not to overuse these products, as they can be drying and irritating to the skin.

For spot treatments, tea tree oil and sulfur products can be effective in reducing the size and redness of pimples.

It's also important to avoid touching or picking at your face, as this can spread bacteria and lead to further breakouts.

In terms of makeup, look for non-comedogenic and oil-free options, and consider using a primer to help control oil production throughout the day.

Overall, it may take some trial and error to find the right combination of products and techniques that work best for your skin, but with patience and consistency, you can improve the appearance of acne-prone skin.

• Skincare tips and products for dry skin

Dry skin can be caused by a lack of moisture in the skin, which can lead to itchiness, flakiness, and rough texture. Here are some skincare tips and products that can help improve dry skin:

1. **Use a gentle cleanser:** Avoid using harsh soaps or cleansers that can strip the skin of its natural oils. Look for a gentle cleanser that won't leave your skin feeling tight or dry.
2. **Moisturize regularly:** Moisturizing is key for dry skin. Look for a moisturizer that contains ingredients like ceramides, hyaluronic acid, or glycerin, which can help hydrate and soothe dry skin.
3. **Exfoliate gently:** Exfoliation can help remove dead skin cells and improve the texture of dry skin. However, be gentle when exfoliating and avoid using harsh scrubs that can irritate the skin. Look for a gentle exfoliating cleanser or a chemical exfoliant with alpha-hydroxy acids (AHAs) or beta-hydroxy acids (BHAs).
4. **Use a face oil:** Face oils can help nourish and hydrate dry skin. Look for oils like jojoba, rosehip, or argan oil, which can help improve skin texture and tone.
5. **Protect your skin:** Protect your skin from the sun's harmful UV rays by using a broad-spectrum sunscreen with at least SPF 30. Sun exposure can further dehydrate dry skin and cause damage.
6. **Use a humidifier:** If you live in a dry climate or during the winter months, consider using a humidifier in your home to add moisture to the air.
7. **Avoid hot showers:** Hot water can strip the skin of its natural oils and make dry skin worse. Try to use lukewarm water when showering or bathing and avoid staying in the water for too

long.

Some products that can be helpful for dry skin include:

- Cetaphil Gentle Skin Cleanser
- Cerave Moisturizing Cream
- The Ordinary Hyaluronic Acid 2% + B5
- Drunk Elephant Virgin Marula Luxury Facial Oil
- La Roche-Posay Anthelios Mineral Sunscreen SPF 50
- First Aid Beauty Ultra Repair Cream

It's important to remember that everyone's skin is different, and what works for one person may not work for another. If you have persistent dry skin or other skin concerns, it's best to consult with a dermatologist.

Dry skin can be uncomfortable and often leads to flaking, itching, and even cracking. Here are some tips and product recommendations for those with dry skin:

1. **Use a gentle, hydrating cleanser:** Avoid using harsh, drying cleansers and instead opt for a gentle, hydrating cleanser that won't strip your skin of its natural oils.
2. **Moisturize regularly:** Moisturizing is crucial for dry skin. Look for a moisturizer that contains hydrating ingredients like hyaluronic acid, glycerin, and ceramides.
3. **Consider using a facial oil:** Facial oils can be a great addition to your skincare routine if you have dry skin. Look for oils that are rich in fatty acids, like argan oil or rosehip oil.
4. **Exfoliate gently:** Exfoliating can help remove dead skin cells and allow your moisturizer to penetrate better. However, be sure to use a gentle exfoliant, like a sugar scrub, and only exfoliate once or twice a week.
5. **Avoid hot showers:** Hot water can strip your skin of its natural oils, leaving it even drier. Stick to lukewarm water

instead.

6. **Use a humidifier:** Dry air can make your skin even drier. Using a humidifier can add moisture to the air and help keep your skin hydrated.

Product recommendations:

- Cetaphil Gentle Skin Cleanser
- Cerave Moisturizing Cream
- The Ordinary 100% Plant-Derived Squalane
- Fresh Sugar Face Polish Exfoliator
- Mario Badescu Facial Spray with Aloe, Herbs, and Rosewater
- Dyson Pure Humidify+Cool

Dry skin can be uncomfortable and irritating, especially during the colder months when the air is drier. Here are some skincare tips and products that can help:

1. **Use a gentle cleanser:** Avoid harsh, drying cleansers that can strip your skin of its natural oils. Look for a gentle, hydrating cleanser that will leave your skin feeling soft and moisturized.
2. **Exfoliate once or twice a week:** Exfoliating can help to remove dead skin cells and promote cell turnover, which can improve the overall texture and appearance of your skin. However, be careful not to over-exfoliate, as this can further dry out your skin.
3. **Moisturize regularly:** Moisturizing is key for dry skin. Look for a rich, hydrating moisturizer that contains ingredients like hyaluronic acid, glycerin, and ceramides. Apply it twice a day, or as needed.
4. **Use a facial oil:** Facial oils can provide an extra layer of hydration and help to seal in moisture. Look for oils that are non-comedogenic, meaning they won't clog your pores.

5. **Drink plenty of water:** Staying hydrated is important for overall skin health, so be sure to drink plenty of water throughout the day.
6. **Consider a humidifier:** If you live in a dry climate or use heating or air conditioning, a humidifier can help to add moisture to the air and prevent your skin from drying out.
7. **Avoid hot showers:** Hot water can further dry out your skin, so try to take lukewarm showers instead.

As for products, look for moisturizers that are specifically formulated for dry skin, such as Cetaphil Moisturizing Cream or Neutrogena Hydro Boost Gel Cream. You may also want to try a facial oil, like The Ordinary 100% Organic Cold-Pressed Rose Hip Seed Oil or Josie Maran 100% Pure Argan Oil.

Using a gentle cleanser and hydrating moisturizer, people with dry skin may benefit from incorporating products that contain ingredients like hyaluronic acid, glycerin, and ceramides. These ingredients can help to attract and retain moisture in the skin, improving its overall hydration. Exfoliating once or twice a week with a mild scrub can also help to remove dead skin cells and improve the skin's texture. Additionally, using a face oil or incorporating facial massage techniques can help to boost circulation and nourish the skin.

• Skincare tips and products for oily skin

If you have oily skin, you're likely to experience excess oil production, enlarged pores, and a shiny appearance. However, with the right skincare routine and products, you can help to control oil production and promote a healthy, balanced complexion. Here are some tips and product recommendations for those with oily skin:

1. **Cleanse your skin twice a day:** Use a gentle, non-comedogenic cleanser to remove dirt, oil, and makeup from your skin. Look for a formula that contains salicylic acid or benzoyl peroxide, which can help to unclog pores and control oil production.

2. **Use a toner:** A toner can help to balance your skin's pH levels and control excess oil. Look for a toner that contains witch hazel or tea tree oil, which have astringent properties that can help to tighten pores.

3. **Moisturize:** Even oily skin needs moisture, so don't skip this step! Look for a lightweight, oil-free moisturizer that won't clog your pores. You can also try a gel moisturizer, which can help to hydrate your skin without leaving a greasy residue.

4. **Use a clay mask:** Clay masks are great for oily skin because they can help to absorb excess oil and impurities from your skin. Look for a mask that contains kaolin or bentonite clay, which can help to unclog pores and reduce shine.

5. **Use a retinoid:** Retinoids, such as retinol, can help to control oil production and improve the appearance of your skin. Look for a product that contains a low percentage of retinol, as higher concentrations can be too harsh for oily skin.

6. **Use oil-free makeup:** If you wear makeup, look for oil-free formulas that won't clog your pores or contribute to excess oil production.

SKINCARE 101: A COMPREHENSIVE GUIDE TO HEALTHY GLOWING SKIN

Remember, even though you have oily skin, it's still important to use sunscreen every day to protect your skin from the sun's harmful UV rays. Look for a lightweight, oil-free formula that won't leave a greasy residue on your skin.

If you have oily skin, it's essential to use products that can help control excess oil production without stripping the skin of its natural moisture. Here are some skincare tips and products that can benefit oily skin:

1. **Use a gentle cleanser:** Choose a gentle, non-comedogenic cleanser that won't clog your pores. Look for ingredients like salicylic acid, which can help regulate oil production and prevent breakouts.
2. **Exfoliate regularly:** Exfoliation can help remove dead skin cells and unclog pores, which can reduce the appearance of oily skin. However, be careful not to over-exfoliate, as this can lead to irritation and further oil production.
3. **Use a toner:** A toner can help remove any remaining dirt or oil from your skin after cleansing. Look for toners that contain ingredients like witch hazel or tea tree oil, which can help control oil production.
4. **Use oil-free moisturizers:** Even if you have oily skin, it's important to moisturize regularly to keep your skin healthy. Look for oil-free moisturizers that won't clog your pores.
5. **Use a clay mask:** Clay masks can help absorb excess oil and impurities from the skin. Look for masks that contain ingredients like bentonite clay, which can help control oil production.
6. **Use sunscreen:** It's important to protect your skin from the sun, even if you have oily skin. Look for lightweight, oil-free sunscreens that won't clog your pores.

Some recommended products for oily skin include:

- Neutrogena Oil-Free Acne Wash
- Paula's Choice Skin Perfecting 2% BHA Liquid Exfoliant
- Thayers Witch Hazel Toner
- La Roche-Posay Effaclar Mat Daily Moisturizer
- Aztec Secret Indian Healing Clay Mask
- EltaMD UV Clear Facial Sunscreen

When it comes to oily skin, the key is to find the right balance between keeping the skin clean and avoiding over-drying it. Here are some additional tips and products that can help:

1. **Use a gentle cleanser:** Choose a cleanser that is specifically formulated for oily skin and that contains ingredients such as salicylic acid or benzoyl peroxide to help control oil production.
2. **Use a toner:** A toner can help remove any remaining traces of dirt or oil after cleansing and can also help to tighten pores. Look for a toner that contains witch hazel, which is a natural astringent.
3. **Moisturize:** Even oily skin needs moisturizing, so look for a lightweight, oil-free moisturizer that won't clog your pores.
4. **Use blotting papers:** If you find that your skin becomes oily throughout the day, use blotting papers to absorb excess oil. Avoid using powder to control oil, as it can make your skin look cakey.
5. **Try a clay mask:** Clay masks can be especially helpful for oily skin, as they can help to draw out impurities and absorb excess oil. Look for masks that contain ingredients such as kaolin clay or bentonite clay.
6. **Avoid touching your face:** Touching your face can transfer dirt and oil from your hands to your skin, which can lead to breakouts. Try to avoid touching your face throughout the day and be sure to wash your hands regularly.

7. **Consider using a retinoid:** Retinoids can help to regulate oil production and keep pores clear. Talk to your dermatologist about whether a retinoid might be a good option for you.

Remember, everyone's skin is different, so it may take some trial and error to find the right products and routine for you. If you're not sure where to start, consider consulting with a dermatologist or skincare professional for personalized advice.

The tips mentioned above, here are some more tips for oily skin:

1. **Use oil-free products:** Look for oil-free or non-comedogenic products to avoid clogging your pores and exacerbating oiliness.
2. **Blotting papers:** Keep blotting papers with you throughout the day to absorb excess oil without disrupting your makeup.
3. **Avoid over-washing:** Over-washing can strip your skin of its natural oils, causing it to produce even more oil to compensate. Stick to washing your face twice a day.
4. **Use a clay mask:** A clay mask can help absorb excess oil and unclog pores.
5. **Exfoliate regularly:** Exfoliating can help remove dead skin cells that can contribute to clogged pores and breakouts.
6. **Use a toner:** A toner can help balance your skin's pH levels and remove any remaining dirt or oil.
7. **Avoid heavy or greasy products:** Heavy or greasy products can make your skin feel even oilier, so opt for lightweight, oil-free options.

Remember, everyone's skin is different, so it may take some trial and error to find the right skincare routine for you. If you have severe or persistent oily skin, consider consulting a dermatologist for personalized recommendations.

• Skincare tips and products for aging skin

As we age, our skin undergoes various changes, including a decrease in collagen production, which can lead to wrinkles, fine lines, and dryness. To keep your skin looking youthful, it's important to use skincare products and routines that target these specific concerns. Here are some tips and recommendations for skincare for aging skin:

1. **Hydration is Key:** As you age, your skin naturally loses moisture, leading to dryness and the appearance of fine lines and wrinkles. Incorporating a moisturizer into your skincare routine can help to combat this. Look for a moisturizer with hydrating ingredients like hyaluronic acid, glycerin, or ceramides.

2. **Retinoids:** Retinoids are a type of vitamin A that can help to stimulate collagen production, reduce fine lines and wrinkles, and improve skin texture. Look for products that contain retinol or retinoids but be sure to start with a low concentration and gradually increase usage to prevent irritation.

3. **Sun Protection:** Sun exposure is a major contributor to aging skin, so it's important to protect your skin from harmful UV rays. Make sure to apply sunscreen with at least SPF 30 daily and wear protective clothing and accessories when spending time in the sun.

4. **Antioxidants:** Antioxidants like vitamin C and E can help to protect the skin from damage caused by free radicals, which can contribute to aging. Look for skincare products that contain antioxidants or add a serum with vitamin C to your routine.

5. **Exfoliation:** As we age, our skin's natural exfoliation process slows down, leading to a buildup of dead skin cells and a dull

complexion. Incorporating an exfoliating product like a gentle scrub or chemical exfoliant into your routine can help to improve skin texture and brightness.

6. **Eye Cream:** The delicate skin around the eyes is often one of the first areas to show signs of aging. Using an eye cream that targets fine lines, wrinkles, and dark circles can help to keep this area looking youthful and bright.

7. **Facial Oils:** Facial oils can help to nourish and hydrate aging skin, as well as improve skin texture and elasticity. Look for oils like argan, rosehip, or marula that are rich in antioxidants and fatty acids.

By incorporating these tips and products into your skincare routine, you can help to keep your skin looking youthful and radiant as you age. However, it's important to remember that everyone's skin is unique, so it may take some experimentation to find the products and routine that work best for you.

As we age, our skin undergoes various changes that can result in fine lines, wrinkles, and sagging. However, there are many ways to address these concerns and keep your skin looking youthful and vibrant.

Some skincare tips for aging skin include:

1. **Use a gentle cleanser:** As we age, our skin becomes thinner and more delicate, so it's important to use a gentle cleanser that won't strip away essential oils.

2. **Moisturize regularly:** Dry skin is more prone to wrinkles and fine lines, so it's important to keep your skin hydrated with a good moisturizer.

3. **Use products with antioxidants:** Antioxidants like vitamin C and E can help protect your skin from free radical damage and promote collagen production.

4. **Wear sunscreen:** Sun damage is one of the primary causes of premature aging, so it's important to protect your skin from

UV rays with a broad-spectrum sunscreen.

5. **Consider using retinoids**: Retinoids are a type of vitamin A that can help improve the appearance of fine lines, wrinkles, and age spots.

6. **Hydrate from the inside out:** Drinking plenty of water and eating a healthy diet rich in fruits and vegetables can help keep your skin looking youthful and healthy.

When it comes to products, some ingredients that can be particularly beneficial for aging skin include hyaluronic acid, peptides, and niacinamide. Additionally, there are many anti-aging serums and creams on the market that can help improve the appearance of fine lines and wrinkles. It's important to find products that work well for your skin type and incorporate them into a consistent skincare routine for best results.

As we age, our skin undergoes changes such as loss of elasticity, fine lines, wrinkles, and dullness. To address these concerns, there are several tips and products that can be incorporated into a skincare routine:

1. **Sunscreen:** Applying sunscreen every day is crucial for protecting your skin from the damaging effects of UV rays, which can cause premature aging.

2. **Retinoids:** Retinoids are a type of vitamin A that can help reduce the appearance of fine lines, wrinkles, and uneven skin tone. They work by increasing cell turnover and collagen production.

3. **Antioxidants:** Antioxidants, such as vitamin C and E, help protect the skin from free radical damage and promote collagen production.

4. **Hydration:** Aging skin tends to be drier, so using a moisturizer that contains ingredients like hyaluronic acid can help plump and hydrate the skin.

5. **Exfoliation:** Regular exfoliation can help remove dead skin

cells and promote cell turnover, resulting in smoother, brighter-looking skin.

6. **Facial massage:** Facial massage can help improve circulation and promote lymphatic drainage, which can help reduce puffiness and improve the overall appearance of the skin.

7. **Eye cream:** The skin around the eyes is delicate and prone to fine lines and wrinkles. Using an eye cream that contains ingredients like caffeine and peptides can help reduce the appearance of under-eye bags and dark circles.

Incorporating these tips and products into a daily skincare routine can help improve the appearance of aging skin and promote a more youthful complexion.

Chapter 6: Skincare Products and Ingredients

• Overview of common skincare products and ingredients

Here is an overview of some common skincare products and ingredients:

1. **Cleansers:** Used to remove dirt, oil, and makeup from the skin. Some common ingredients in cleansers include glycerin, salicylic acid, and benzoyl peroxide.
2. **Toners:** Used to balance the skin's pH level after cleansing and can also help to tighten and refine pores. Common ingredients in toners include witch hazel, rosewater, and glycolic acid.
3. **Serums:** A lightweight, highly concentrated product that delivers active ingredients deep into the skin. Common ingredients in serums include vitamin C, hyaluronic acid, and retinol.
4. **Moisturizers:** Used to hydrate and protect the skin, and can come in various formulations, such as creams, lotions, and gels. Common ingredients in moisturizers include ceramides, glycerin, and shea butter.
5. **Sunscreen:** Used to protect the skin from the harmful effects of UV rays, which can cause premature aging and skin cancer. Common ingredients in sunscreens include zinc oxide, titanium dioxide, and avobenzone.
6. **Exfoliants:** Used to remove dead skin cells and improve skin texture. Common ingredients in exfoliants include alpha-hydroxy acids (AHAs) and beta-hydroxy acids (BHAs).
7. **Masks:** Used to provide a deep cleanse, hydrate, or brighten the skin. Common ingredients in masks include clay, charcoal,

and vitamin C.

These are just some of the many skincare products and ingredients available. It's important to choose products that are suitable for your skin type and address your specific concerns.

Common skincare products include cleansers, toners, moisturizers, serums, and sunscreens. Cleansers are used to remove dirt, oil, and makeup from the skin. Toners help to balance the skin's pH and prepare it for moisturization. Moisturizers hydrate the skin and prevent moisture loss. Serums are concentrated products that target specific skin concerns, such as wrinkles or dark spots. Sunscreens protect the skin from harmful UV rays that can cause skin damage and aging.

Ingredients commonly found in skincare products include retinol, vitamin C, hyaluronic acid, glycolic acid, and salicylic acid. Retinol is a form of vitamin A that promotes cell turnover and collagen production, helping to reduce the appearance of wrinkles and fine lines. Vitamin C is an antioxidant that brightens the skin and helps to even out skin tone. Hyaluronic acid is a humectant that draws moisture to the skin, providing hydration and plumping effects. Glycolic acid and salicylic acid are exfoliants that help to unclog pores and remove dead skin cells.

There are numerous skincare products and ingredients available on the market, each with their own unique properties and benefits. Some of the most common skincare products include cleansers, toners, serums, moisturizers, and sunscreens.

Cleansers are designed to remove dirt, oil, and impurities from the skin. They come in a variety of formulations, such as foaming, gel, cream, or oil cleansers, and can be used in the morning and at night.

Toners are typically used after cleansing to balance the skin's pH and remove any leftover residue. They can also provide additional benefits, such as hydration, exfoliation, or calming the skin.

Serums are lightweight, fast-absorbing liquids that contain high concentrations of active ingredients. They are typically used after toning and before moisturizing to address specific skin concerns, such as brightening, anti-aging, or hydration.

Moisturizers are designed to hydrate and protect the skin. They can come in different formulations, such as creams, lotions, or gels, and should be used both in the morning and at night to keep the skin supple and soft.

Sunscreens are crucial for protecting the skin from harmful UV rays, which can lead to premature aging and skin cancer. They come in different forms, such as lotions, creams, sprays, or powders, and should be applied every day, even when it's cloudy or raining.

Some common skincare ingredients include:

- Hyaluronic acid: A humectant that can hold up to 1,000 times its weight in water, making it a popular ingredient for hydrating the skin.
- Retinoids: A derivative of vitamin A that can help reduce the appearance of fine lines, wrinkles, and dark spots.
- Vitamin C: A potent antioxidant that can brighten the skin, even out the skin tone, and protect against environmental stressors.
- Salicylic acid: A beta-hydroxy acid that can help exfoliate the skin and unclog pores, making it a popular ingredient for treating acne-prone skin.
- Niacinamide: A form of vitamin B3 that can help reduce inflammation, improve skin elasticity, and regulate oil production.

It's important to note that while many skincare products and ingredients can be beneficial, not every product will work for every person. It's important to pay attention to your skin's unique needs and adjust your skincare routine accordingly.

Common skincare products and ingredients can vary greatly depending on the individual's skin type, concerns, and personal preferences. However, some of the most commonly used products include cleansers, toners, serums, moisturizers, and sunscreens.

Cleansers come in various forms such as foaming, gel, cream, or oil-based and are used to remove dirt, oil, and makeup from the skin. Toners can help balance the skin's pH level, tighten pores, and provide additional hydration. Serums are typically lightweight and contain high concentrations of active ingredients such as vitamins, antioxidants, and hyaluronic acid to target specific concerns like fine lines, hyperpigmentation, or dullness. Moisturizers can come in various forms such as creams, lotions, or gels, and are used to hydrate and protect the skin barrier. Lastly, sunscreens are essential for protecting the skin from UV damage and should be used daily, even on cloudy days.

Some common ingredients found in skincare products include retinoids, vitamin C, glycolic acid, salicylic acid, niacinamide, and ceramides. Retinoids are a form of vitamin A and can help improve the appearance of fine lines, wrinkles, and uneven texture. Vitamin C is a powerful antioxidant that can help brighten the skin and reduce hyperpigmentation. Glycolic acid and salicylic acid are types of exfoliants that can help unclog pores and improve skin texture. Niacinamide is a form of vitamin B3 that can help reduce inflammation and redness. Ceramides are lipids that can help strengthen the skin barrier and improve hydration.

It's important to note that not all products and ingredients work for everyone, and it's essential to patch test new products and consult with a dermatologist if experiencing any adverse reactions or concerns.

• How to choose the right products for your skin type and concerns

To choose the right skincare products for your skin type and concerns, it's important to first determine your skin type (dry, oily, combination, sensitive, etc.) and understand your specific skincare concerns (acne, aging, hyperpigmentation, etc.). Once you have this information, you can look for products that are formulated for your skin type and target your specific concerns.

When selecting skincare products, it's also important to pay attention to the ingredients. Look for products with ingredients that are known to be beneficial for your skin type and concerns, such as hyaluronic acid for dry skin, salicylic acid for acne-prone skin, and retinol for anti-aging. Be wary of products that contain harsh or potentially irritating ingredients, such as alcohol, fragrances, and sulfates.

It's also a good idea to read product reviews and seek recommendations from trusted sources, such as dermatologists or skincare experts. Don't be afraid to experiment with different products to find what works best for your skin. However, it's important to introduce new products gradually and patch test them first to avoid any potential allergic reactions or irritation.

When choosing skincare products, it's important to consider your skin type and specific concerns. For example, if you have oily skin, you may want to look for products that are oil-free or labeled as "matte" or "oil-control." If you have dry skin, you may want to look for products that contain moisturizing ingredients like hyaluronic acid or glycerin.

In addition to considering your skin type, it's important to read the labels and ingredient lists of products. Look for ingredients that are known to be effective for your specific concerns. For example, if you're looking for a product to help reduce the appearance of fine lines and wrinkles, you may want to look for products that contain retinol or peptides.

It's also a good idea to research and read reviews of products before purchasing them. You can look for reviews on retailer websites or search for reviews from trusted beauty bloggers or influencers. Additionally, you may want to consult with a dermatologist or esthetician to get personalized recommendations based on your specific skin concerns.

• Understanding labels and ingredients lists

Understanding the labels and ingredients lists of skincare products can help you choose products that are appropriate for your skin type and concerns. Here are some key terms and ingredients to look out for:

1. **Active ingredients:** These are the ingredients that make up the bulk of the product and provide the desired benefits. Look for active ingredients that are effective for your skin type and concerns.
2. **Inactive ingredients:** These are the ingredients that are added to the product for texture, consistency, and preservation. They can include emulsifiers, preservatives, and thickeners.
3. **Fragrance:** Fragrances can be derived from natural or synthetic sources. However, they can be irritating for some people, especially those with sensitive skin. Look for fragrance-free products or those with natural fragrances.
4. **Natural and organic:** These terms are not regulated, so it's important to read the label carefully and check the ingredients list. Look for products that contain certified organic ingredients or are certified by a reputable organization.
5. **Preservatives:** Preservatives are added to prevent the growth of bacteria and other microorganisms. Look for preservatives that are considered safe and effective.
6. **Sunscreen:** Look for broad-spectrum sunscreen with an SPF of 30 or higher. The active ingredients should be titanium dioxide or zinc oxide, which are considered safe and effective.
7. **pH:** The pH of a skincare product is important because it can affect the skin's natural pH. Look for products with a pH that is similar to the skin's natural pH (around 5.5).
8. **Allergens:** Look out for common allergens like peanuts, tree

nuts, and gluten if you have allergies.

9. **Irritants:** Certain ingredients like alcohol, retinoids, and alpha-hydroxy acids can be irritating for some people. If you have sensitive skin, look for products that are formulated for sensitive skin.

By understanding the labels and ingredients lists of skincare products, you can make informed choices and choose products that are appropriate for your skin type and concerns.

Understanding labels and ingredients lists is crucial to make informed decisions about the skincare products we use. Here are some important things to keep in mind when reading labels and ingredients lists:

1. **Ingredients are listed in descending order:** The first ingredient listed is the most prevalent in the product, while the last is the least. This means that if a product claims to contain a specific ingredient but it's listed at the end, it's likely there in small amounts.

2. **Know the difference between active and inactive ingredients:** Active ingredients are those that have been clinically proven to have an effect on the skin, such as salicylic acid for acne or retinol for anti-aging. Inactive ingredients, on the other hand, are those that don't have any direct effect on the skin but serve other functions, such as preservatives or thickeners.

3. **Be aware of potential irritants:** Certain ingredients, such as fragrances, alcohol, and some essential oils, can be irritating to some skin types. If you have sensitive skin, it's best to avoid products that contain these ingredients.

4. **Research unfamiliar ingredients:** If you come across an ingredient you've never heard of before, take the time to research it and understand its purpose and potential effects on

the skin. Websites such as Paula's Choice or EWG's Skin Deep can be helpful resources.

5. **Don't rely on marketing claims:** Skincare products often make bold claims about their effectiveness, but it's important to look beyond the marketing and understand the actual ingredients and their concentrations to determine if a product is likely to work for your skin concerns.

By understanding labels and ingredients lists, we can make informed decisions about the products we use and ensure that they are safe and effective for our individual skin types and concerns.

Understanding labels and ingredients lists is essential for choosing the right skincare products for your skin type and concerns. Here are some things to keep in mind:

1. **Look for key active ingredients:** The first five ingredients on a label make up the majority of the product, so make sure they contain key active ingredients that address your specific skin concerns.
2. Avoid harsh or irritating ingredients: Check for ingredients like alcohol, sulfates, and fragrances that can be harsh or irritating to the skin, especially if you have sensitive skin.
3. **Be aware of preservatives:** Preservatives are necessary to prevent bacterial growth in skincare products, but some can be harsh or allergenic. Look for gentler preservatives like phenoxyethanol or potassium sorbate.
4. **Consider your skin type:** Choose products that are formulated for your skin type, whether it is dry, oily, combination, or sensitive.
5. Research unfamiliar ingredients: If you come across an unfamiliar ingredient, do some research to determine its purpose and potential effects on the skin.
6. **Beware of marketing claims:** Be wary of marketing claims like

"all-natural" or "organic," as they do not necessarily mean a product is better or safer for the skin. It is important to still read the ingredients list and do your research.

By understanding labels and ingredients lists, you can make informed decisions about the skincare products you use and ensure they are effective and safe for your skin.

Conclusion: The importance of self-care and consistent skincare routine for healthy skin

Self-care and a consistent skincare routine are essential for healthy and beautiful skin. A good skincare routine can help you maintain the health and appearance of your skin by keeping it hydrated, nourished, and protected from external aggressors.

Self-care involves taking time to care for yourself and your skin, both physically and emotionally. This may include taking a relaxing bath, practicing yoga or meditation, getting enough sleep, eating a healthy diet, and managing stress.

A consistent skincare routine is also important, as it helps your skin get the regular care it needs to stay healthy. This involves cleansing your skin daily, moisturizing to keep it hydrated, using sunscreen to protect it from harmful UV rays, and using targeted treatments to address any specific concerns or issues.

When it comes to skincare, it's also important to listen to your skin and adjust your routine as needed. This may involve trying new products or techniques or seeking the advice of a skincare professional.

Self-care and a consistent skincare routine are essential for maintaining healthy, beautiful skin and promoting a sense of well-being and self-confidence.

Consistent skincare and self-care practices are essential for maintaining healthy skin. A good skincare routine can help to prevent or address various skin concerns, such as acne, dryness, or wrinkles, and promote a radiant and youthful complexion. Self-care practices, such as stress management, adequate sleep, and a healthy diet, can also impact the health and appearance of the skin.

In addition to the physical benefits, skincare and self-care practices can also have mental and emotional benefits. Taking time to care for oneself can promote relaxation, reduce stress, and improve overall well-being. Additionally, having a consistent skincare routine can be a form of self-care and an opportunity to practice mindfulness and self-reflection.

Prioritizing self-care and skincare practices can help to promote healthy and glowing skin, as well as physical and mental well-being.

Consistency is key when it comes to taking care of your skin. A daily skincare routine, along with healthy lifestyle habits, can help maintain and improve the overall health and appearance of your skin. Self-care is also an important aspect of a healthy skincare routine, as it can help reduce stress levels and improve your overall well-being.

When you take care of your skin consistently, you may start to see improvements in the texture, tone, and overall health of your skin. By following a consistent routine and using the right products for your skin type and concerns, you can help prevent common skin problems and reduce the signs of aging.

In addition to a daily skincare routine, it's important to also prioritize self-care practices such as staying hydrated, getting enough sleep, and managing stress levels. This can help support healthy skin from the inside out and enhance the benefits of your skincare routine.

Having a consistent skincare routine is essential for healthy skin as it helps to maintain its natural balance and protect it from environmental factors that can cause damage. Additionally, taking the time to care for your skin can also be a form of self-care, promoting relaxation and reducing stress. Self-care practices have been shown to have a positive impact on mental health and well-being, making skincare a small but significant way to prioritize your overall health. By understanding your skin type and concerns and selecting the right products for your needs, you can establish a routine that works for you and helps to promote healthy, glowing skin.

In conclusion, taking care of your skin is important for both your physical health and your self-confidence. By adopting a consistent skincare routine, using the right products for your skin type and concerns, and paying attention to lifestyle factors that affect your skin, you can improve the health and appearance of your skin.

Remember that self-care goes beyond just skincare products. It's important to prioritize sleep, hydration, a healthy diet, and stress management in order to support your overall health and wellbeing, which will also have a positive impact on your skin.

With the right approach and a little bit of patience, you can achieve healthy, radiant skin that makes you feel confident and beautiful.

A consistent skincare routine that includes cleansing, moisturizing, and protecting your skin can help maintain its natural beauty and prevent damage caused by external factors. Understanding your skin type and concerns can help you choose the right products and ingredients to address them. Additionally, incorporating self-care practices such as staying hydrated, getting enough sleep, and managing stress can also contribute to healthier skin. Remember, healthy skin is a reflection of your overall health and well-being, so make self-care and skincare a priority in your daily routine.

Using high-quality products that suit our individual skin type and concerns, can help us maintain healthy, radiant, and youthful-looking skin. It is also crucial to incorporate self-care practices, such as staying hydrated, eating a healthy diet, getting enough sleep, and managing stress, to promote skin health from within. By prioritizing our skincare and self-care, we can not only achieve healthy skin but also feel more confident and comfortable in our own skin.

Don't miss out!

Visit the website below and you can sign up to receive emails whenever Masonwabe Nyanga publishes a new book. There's no charge and no obligation.

https://books2read.com/r/B-A-QPKX-KPIIC

BOOKS 2 READ

Connecting independent readers to independent writers.

Did you love *Skincare 101: A Comprehensive Guide to Healthy Glowing Skin*? Then you should read *Shining Light on Darkness: A Journey to Healing From Depression*[1] by Masonwabe Nyanga!

[2]

Shining Light on Darkness: A Journey to Healing from Depression is a comprehensive guide to understanding and overcoming depression. Author Masonwabe Nyanga shares his own journey of healing and provides practical strategies and tools for those struggling with depression.

This book covers a range of topics including identifying symptoms, seeking professional help, developing healthy coping mechanisms, and exploring alternative therapies. Nyanga also provides insights into the underlying causes of depression, including societal pressures, trauma, and genetics.

---

1. https://books2read.com/u/bW0w1D

2. https://books2read.com/u/bW0w1D

With a compassionate and relatable tone, Shining Light on Darkness offers hope and guidance to anyone who is struggling with depression. Whether you are experiencing depression for the first time or have been living with it for years, this book will provide you with the tools and knowledge you need to begin your journey to healing.

Table of Contents